# S.O.S.
## Save Our Stream

By Judy Nayer

Illustrated by Thea Kliros

**Modern Curriculum Press**
*Parsippany, New Jersey*

Cover and book design by John Maddalone

ISBN 0-7652-2168-3

Printed in the United States of America

4 5 6 7 8 9 10    07 06 05 04 03

Modern
Curriculum
Press

Pearson Learning Group

**1-800-321-3106**
**www.pearsonlearning.com**

# **Contents**

**Chapter 1**
The Field Trip . . . . . . . . . . . . . . . . . . . page 5

**Chapter 2**
The Experiments . . . . . . . . . . . . . . . page 15

**Chapter 3**
Steve's Big Idea . . . . . . . . . . . . . . . . page 22

**Chapter 4**
Adopting the Stream . . . . . . . . . . . . . page 33

**Chapter 5**
Clean-Up Day . . . . . . . . . . . . . . . . . page 41

**Chapter 6**
Spreading the News . . . . . . . . . . . . . page 51

**Chapter 7**
More Good News . . . . . . . . . . . . . . . page 57

**Glossary** . . . . . . . . . . . . . . . . . . . . . page 64

For Matthew,
and for "earth keepers"
everywhere

# Chapter 1

# The Field Trip

On a sunny Friday in spring, Steve Alvarez was so excited that he ran all the way to school. Friday was his favorite day. First of all, it meant that tomorrow was Saturday, when Steve and his parents usually did something special together. On Fridays his teacher, Mrs. Delgado, also gave them a free hour at the end of the day to read or draw or do whatever they liked.

Today was an extra special Friday. Mrs. Delgado was taking the class on a field trip. She was being very mysterious about it, too. All they'd been told was that the field trip would take place during science class and that they would stay near the school.

Steve loved science. Instead of using their regular classroom, the class went to a special science laboratory. Mrs. Delgado had all kinds of interesting rocks, shells, fossils, eggs, and bones in the room. There were cages, aquariums, and terrariums full of frogs, bugs, snakes, fish, mice, and gerbils, too.

Steve loved animals. He had five pets of his own—two goldfish, a snail he had found in the backyard, a parakeet, and a hamster. He wanted to work with animals when he grew up. He thought he might be a veterinarian or even a park ranger.

When Steve's class got to the science room that Friday, Mrs. Delgado had them form into groups of four. Steve joined his best friends Luke Williams, Wendy Asato, and Karen Harper. They were all in Mrs. Delgado's after-school Ecology Club, called EcoKids, and they were all excited about the field trip.

"Where do you think we're going on this field trip?" Steve asked his friends.

"I don't know," Karen said. "The paper we brought home last week for our parents to sign didn't say much about it. A lot of places are within walking distance of the school."

Mrs. Delgado led the students out of the classroom. They went down the stairs and out the door of the school. Still, she wouldn't tell them exactly where they were going. "You'll see," she kept saying whenever anyone asked.

They walked behind the school and through the parking lot. Beyond the parking lot was a grassy area, and beyond that stood a tall metal fence with a locked gate. None of the kids had ever been beyond the fence.

Mrs. Delgado took a large key from her pocket. She wiggled it in the lock for a few seconds, and when it clicked, she pushed the gate open. "Go through one at a time," she told them, "and wait for me to pull the gate closed."

"Cool," Steve said, "we're going to hike somewhere." When he and his friends had gone through the fence, they found themselves at the top of a trail leading down a small hill.

The class followed as Mrs. Delgado led them down the dirt trail. The path ended at the bottom of the hill. What they found there was completely unexpected.

A muddy-looking creek flowed down from the woods, but it couldn't go farther than the small clearing where the path ended. A dam of litter blocked the creek. There were bottles, cans, and cups floating in the greasy water, a bunch of old balloons tied with worn-out ribbon, dirty plastic bags, an old tire, and other junk. Everyone in the class stared at the garbage.

"Yuck," Steve couldn't help saying.

"What is all this?" Wendy asked.

"This, boys and girls," answered Mrs. Delgado, "is the middle of a stream called Silver Creek."

"It doesn't look like a stream," said Steve. "It looks like a garbage dump. How did all this junk get here?"

"It does look like a garbage dump," Mrs. Delgado agreed. "Unfortunately, there are irresponsible people who actually dump their trash in streams like this one."

"Why would anyone do that?" Karen asked.

"Well," said Mrs. Delgado, "I think some people just toss their garbage any place. They don't realize that what they're doing can pollute the water supply," Mrs. Delgado continued.

"You mean all of this trash can get into the town's water?" asked Luke.

"Rivers, lakes, and streams are all connected," Mrs. Delgado told them.

"When my dad and I go hiking, we sometimes take the trail that goes along the Flint River to the reservoir. That's the lake that supplies all the town's water. So junk like this *can* get into the water we drink!" Steve said.

"Maybe people dump their trash here because the stream is so muddy-looking," Luke suggested. "Maybe they figure it's already dirty here, so it doesn't matter."

"Maybe," Mrs. Delgado said, "but I used to come here when I was little. Back then it was a beautiful, clear stream. It was called Silver Creek because of all the silver-colored trout that swam through it. I haven't seen a trout here in years."

It was hard for the class to imagine that the muddy, junk-filled water they were looking at had ever been a clear stream full of healthy fish. Mrs. Delgado explained that the damage took years. The stream had become polluted not only with trash but with toxins, too. These were poisonous chemicals such as oil, detergent, fertilizers, and pesticides.

"How do all those chemicals get into the stream?" Karen wanted to know.

"Let's go back to the science room and do some experiments," Mrs. Delgado said. "I think that's the best way to answer your question."

When they got to the science room, they noticed that Mrs. Delgado had a number of objects laid out on a big counter. There were three clear plastic buckets of water, and a bunch of smaller things, including small plastic containers, paint, cups, and papers.

# The Experiments

"OK," Mrs. Delgado said, "who remembers what we saw in the creek?"

Wendy raised her hand. "I saw some old plastic containers. One was an empty bleach bottle, and one was from motor oil."

"Good," Mrs. Delgado told her. She held up two small plastic cups. "Let's pretend these are the bottles you saw, Wendy."

Following Mrs. Delgado's directions, Wendy poured some blue paint into one cup. Then she poured yellow paint into the other. Last, she emptied both cups back into the paint jars.

"Are the cups empty?" Mrs. Delgado asked.

Now Steve raised his hand. "Not really," he answered. "There are still some drops of paint in the cups."

Mrs. Delgado nodded. "Very observant, Steve. Now, Wendy, drop one cup into this pail," she said, pointing to one of the buckets of water.

Wendy chose the blue cup and dropped it in. As the cup floated and then sank, everyone could see blue paint swirling into the water. The water wasn't clear anymore.

When Wendy dropped the yellow cup into the same pail, they all saw swirls of yellow start to mix in. Where a yellow swirl met a blue swirl it turned green. Now the water really looked strange. It was a cloudy mix of all three colors.

"I get it," Karen said.

"Go ahead, Karen," Mrs. Delgado said. "See if you can explain what happened."

"Well, the traces of chemicals that are left in the containers people throw into the stream float out into the water. As more and more garbage ends up in the water, more and more chemicals start to mix together in the water."

The class did other experiments, using the clean pails of water that were left. In one experiment, they painted different colors on sheets of paper and let them dry. Later they dropped the papers into one of the buckets.

As the water soaked into the paper, the paint started to spread through the water. This experiment showed how chemicals in printed paper could get into water.

In another experiment, Steve washed a miniature car with soap in one container of water. Then he dumped some paint into another container. Finally, he poured a brown fluid that turned out to be motor oil into a third container. Then, one by one, he dumped all of the containers into the last bucket of clean water.

"When people wash their cars, the soapy water goes into the street, flows down into the storm drain, and into the underground water. When people empty paint cans or pour old motor oil into the storm drains, the same thing happens," Mrs. Delgado said.

"What happens when people put weed killer on their lawns?" Steve asked.

"If it rains, the rain water carries some of the weed killer down into the drains," Mrs. Delgado told him. She sighed. "When there are too many chemicals in the water, it becomes unhealthy and animals such as fish and frogs can't live in it anymore."

It made Steve unhappy to think about the animals' homes becoming polluted.

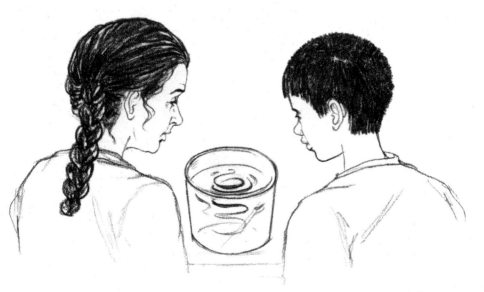

"Well, I hope you came away from our field trip with lots of ideas for a project for our environmental unit," Mrs. Delgado told the class. "You may split up into teams of two to four, and be ready to report on your project in front of the whole class in three weeks."

Since it was Friday, Steve, Luke, Wendy, and Karen used their free hour at the end of the day to get together and talk. "I think we should do our project on Silver Creek," Steve said.

"I don't see how writing a report will help," Luke said. "What can four kids do, anyway?"

"Kids can do a lot. *We* can do a lot," Wendy reminded him.

"Mrs. Delgado said the creek is over three miles long," Karen pointed out. "That's a lot of creek for four people to cover!"

By the time school was over, the kids had agreed on only one thing. Their project would have *something* to do with Silver Creek.

# Chapter 3

# Steve's Big Idea

Steve woke up early on Saturday. He had a lot to do. This was the day he cleaned his hamster's cage and the birdcage and changed the water in the fish tank. As he worked, Steve thought about Silver Creek and the fish that used to live there. He knew his pets wouldn't like it if their homes were dirty.

When he was through with his chores, Steve put on his hiking boots and packed his backpack. Steve's family worked almost every day and evening at the restaurant they owned. Saturday mornings were set aside for doing other things. Today, Steve and his dad were going on a nature hike.

As they drove to nearby Big Mountain Park, Steve told his dad about the field trip to Silver Creek. "Have you ever been to Silver Creek?" he asked his dad.

"Yes," answered Steve's dad, "Papa Tito and I used to fish there all the time. I didn't realize it was as bad as you say, though. I haven't been down there in years."

"Dad, what can we do about it?" Steve asked. "The creek looks terrible, and the garbage may be getting into the town's water supply."

They had just pulled into the parking lot. Steve's dad turned to him and said, "I know this is important, Steve. Let's think about it while we hike, then talk about it later." Steve nodded.

2.3 MILES TO HAWKS PEAK

They gathered their backpacks and headed up the trail. The sign said *2.3 miles to Hawks Peak*. At the top they stopped for a while, enjoying the terrific view of the valley below.

They found a place to sit and had something to eat. Steve was careful to put the garbage in his backpack so he could throw it away later. He always followed the hiker's motto: *Take nothing but pictures. Leave nothing but footprints*. He couldn't imagine just tossing garbage on the ground.

After they finished eating, Steve and his dad decided to hike down a different trail on the way back. They chose the Ladder Falls trail, which wound its way past a small waterfall. Steve always loved to watch the rushing water.

When they got to the point where the trail crossed close to Ladder Falls, Steve was shocked. It wasn't nearly as bad as Silver Creek, but there was more litter around the area than Steve had ever seen before.

"Dad!" he cried. "We have to clean this up!"

"Hold on a minute, Steve," his father told him. "I know you want to go pick up all that trash, but it's not safe just to pick up garbage. We'll tell the park ranger on our way out."

"All this litter is out of control," Steve told his dad on the way home. "It's time for somebody to do something and that somebody is me!"

"Come up with a plan, and I'll help you in anyway I can," Mr. Alvarez said.

"Thanks, Dad!" Steve said.

When he got home, Steve called his friends and told them about the hike and the litter.

"I think the best thing we could do is to figure out a way to clean up Silver Creek," Steve said. "We can at least get rid of some of the trash that's there. We have to start somewhere."

"I guess you're right," Luke agreed. "Anything we can do is better than nothing."

"We could take pictures of the stream before and after we clean it up and make them part of our project," Wendy said.

"Since we'll still have to do some kind of report, why don't we get some facts about water pollution at the library?" Karen suggested. They agreed to meet at the library where Karen's dad was the head librarian.

Karen used the library computer to find books about cleaning up the environment. She copied a few titles in her notebook. Then the kids went to the shelves to find the books.

"Listen to this," Steve said. He read from a fat book called *All About Water*. "Many of the lakes, streams, and rivers in the United States are polluted."

"Wow!" Luke said. "That makes it more important than ever to save Silver Creek."

Later in the afternoon, Mr. Harper came by and said he'd drive them home. Steve checked out a few books to take with him.

29

When Steve got home, his brothers, Rick and Ben, were having a snack in the kitchen. Steve sat down and joined them.

"What's with all the books?" Rick asked.

"We're doing our environmental science project on Silver Creek," Steve told them. "So I checked out some books on water pollution. We thought it might help if we could pick up some of the trash that's there, but it's a *big* job."

"Where's Silver Creek?" Ben asked.

Steve told him about the place behind the school. "No one cares about the creek anymore, so it just keeps getting dirtier and dirtier," Steve said.

"I saw a news story on TV about a town that organized a beach cleanup to get rid of litter," Rick said. "They put up posters asking for volunteers to show up on a certain day, and then they all picked up the trash together. Maybe you could do something like that."

"That's it!" Steve said. "If people help us, we can get Silver Creek cleaned up in no time!"

"Can I help?" asked Ben.

"Sure!" said Steve. "Everyone can."

Later on, Steve told his mom and dad about the idea. "I'll tell you what," said his dad, "we'll supply the garbage bags you'll need to put the trash in. That way we'll be helping, too."

"Thanks, Dad," said Steve. "Wait until I tell my friends!"

# Chapter 4

# **Adopting the Stream**

On Sunday, Steve was too busy to do much about his idea. He had soccer practice in the early afternoon. Then he spent the rest of the day at his family's restaurant. They were preparing a special dinner for his grandfather's birthday. Papa Tito was 65. The guests arrived at four o'clock, and the celebration continued into the evening.

On Monday, Steve told his friends about his idea to hold a stream cleanup day.

"Do you think we need to get special permission from someone?" Karen wondered.

"Let's ask Mrs. Delgado," Steve said.

Later, in science class, everyone broke up into small groups. When Mrs. Delgado came over to talk to the kids about their project, Steve told her, "We don't just want to write a report about Silver Creek. We want to clean it."

"We want to organize a trash cleanup where everyone can help," added Wendy.

"That's a great idea," Mrs. Delgado told them. "In fact, I was thinking of asking Mrs. Jeffers about getting the whole school to adopt the stream. It sounds like you're way ahead of me!" Mrs. Jeffers was the principal of their school.

"Adopt the stream?" asked Steve. "What do you mean?"

"Well," said Mrs. Delgado, "you know what it means to adopt something, right?"

"Yes," said Steve. "I adopted my bird."

"Yes, and when you adopted your bird," she continued, "you had to take care of it, right? Adopting a stream means the same thing—taking care of it and giving it the attention it needs. Because you're taking responsibility for the stream, you will be the stream's caretakers, acting like parents."

The kids laughed at the idea of being parents of a stream, but they were also excited. Karen got paper to make a list.

"My parents said they would supply garbage bags for the clean-up," Steve said. "They also told us we have to wear long pants, long-sleeved shirts, and work boots, and bring a first aid kit. Can you think of anything else we need?"

"Lots of people!" Mrs. Delgado replied. "There's more garbage than you think in Silver Creek. You're also going to need people with cars and trucks to haul it away and dispose of it properly. That means you'll need adults to help. We'll also have to call someone at the town hall. The land behind the school where the creek runs is city property. We need to let the city know what we plan to do and find out where we can dump what we clean up."

"How about Saturday morning?" suggested Luke.

"I think Saturday is perfect," Mrs. Delgado said. "Be sure to put up a notice to tell everyone."

That afternoon, Steve asked his brother if he would help him use the computer. Rick helped Steve write a notice about the cleanup.

It took a while to get the words just right. At last Steve was satisfied. He printed one copy, then rode his bike over to Luke's house to show it to him. The notice said

S.O.S. means "Help"!
It also stands for Save Our Stream!
Children, parents, friends, neighbors—
help us clean up Silver Creek.
Where: Silver Creek
behind the River City School
When: Saturday, April 8, 9 A.M. to 11 A.M.
Garbage bags will be provided.

"Wow!" Luke said. "This looks really professional. This S.O.S. part is great, too."

Steve felt proud. "I wanted to get people's attention," he explained. "The S.O.S. made sense because it's a call for help if a ship is in trouble on the water."

Luke grinned. "It also stands for Save Our Stream. Now our group has a name, too."

"Want to come back to my house to print more copies?" asked Steve.

"Sure!" said Luke. "I'll call my mom." Luke called his mother at the lab where she worked as a scientist. In a few minutes he was off the phone. "I told her about our cleanup project," he told Steve, "and she said we should wear rubber gloves when we pick up the trash. She's going to donate 100 pairs!"

When the boys got back to Steve's house, they made one correction to the notice. They changed the last line to read, "Garbage bags and rubber gloves will be provided."

Later that day and the next, the kids posted notices in the school, at the Alvarez's restaurant, at the library, and at several stores around town. They always made sure they got permission first, but no one said no. Steve and his friends wondered how many people would come to the cleanup. There was nothing to do but wait and see.

# Clean-Up Day

Early the next Saturday, Steve and his family drove to the stream. They parked on the roadside and walked down one of the trails that led to the clearing. Steve's dad remembered the trail from when he was a boy. Everyone carried garbage bags.

At 8:30 A.M., Steve and his family were the first ones there. Soon Luke, his sister Susan, and their mother, Dr. Williams, arrived, followed shortly by Wendy and Mr. Asato. Mr. Asato was wearing long rubber boots he called waders so that he could walk in the water to pick up trash.

Karen and Mrs. Harper showed up a few minutes later. It was still early, but Steve worried. What if they were the only ones?

While they waited, Wendy took pictures of the littered creek. At nine o'clock, Mrs. Delgado showed up with eight other students. They all waited a while longer, but no one else came.

"I guess we'd better get started," Steve said. He was disappointed there weren't more people. He handed out garbage bags and rubber gloves. Then everyone got to work. They picked up all sorts of junk. Things that were recyclable, such as glass, plastic, and aluminum, were separated to take to the recycling center in town later on.

After an hour or so, Steve's back began to hurt from all the bending. His arms started to ache from the heavy sack he pulled along to put all the garbage in. His friends didn't look any happier than he was.

Nearby, Wendy groaned as she stretched to reach a plastic bag caught in a tree branch. "This is hard work!" she called.

"Yeah," Steve said sadly. "If only we had more people. I can't believe no one cares about this place enough to spend a few hours helping us clean it up."

By 11 o'clock everyone was exhausted, and it was time to quit. There was still a lot of garbage left in the creek, but it would just have to wait.

Mrs. Delgado came over and patted Steve on the back. "Don't get discouraged," she said. "It's going to take a lot to undo all the damage that's been caused. You didn't expect to clean up the creek in one day, did you?"

Actually, Steve and the other kids *had* hoped to clean up the creek in one day. No one wanted to admit that to Mrs. Delgado, though.

"We have sandwiches back at the restaurant to help everyone build up their strength again," said Mr. Alvarez. "Who wants to join us?"

Steve, Luke, Karen, and Wendy were the only kids who could go.  Soon they were sitting around a huge pile of sandwiches at the restaurant.

While they ate, they tried to figure out what went wrong. They all knew one thing for sure. They were not giving up.

"Maybe we should try again next Saturday," Karen suggested.

"We could," Steve agreed, "but with only a few people, we're going to have to go there every Saturday for weeks. My dad won't always be able to help either, but I don't want to stop."

"OK, we'll do it every Saturday," Luke said, while Wendy nodded. They all agreed.

They would need new notices, but all they'd have to do was change the date to read, "Every Saturday."

The next Saturday there were even fewer people. Steve, Luke, Karen, and Wendy came early with Mrs. Asato. Everyone else's parents were too busy that day. When Mrs. Delgado pulled up in the parking area, she was alone.

Everyone started down the trail to the creek. Then Steve suddenly saw something. There were people down by the creek. He didn't recognize them, so he scrambled down the path to make sure they had gloves and bags.

As he got closer to the creek, Steve heard a metallic clattering sound. Then he saw two people running away through the trees. When Steve got to the creek and saw why, he felt like crying.

"I can't believe it," Steve exploded. As the others caught up, they saw why he was so angry. A burst-open garbage bag lay in the water. Spread all around it were dozens of paint cans. They could see blue paint already leaking out of one can.

"Those people weren't here to help at all," Steve said sadly. "Why would anyone do this?"

Mrs. Delgado sighed. "Most towns, River City included, have laws against throwing things like empty paint cans, used motor oil, and batteries in regular garbage because of possible pollution. Some people don't want to bring this stuff to special dumping places or pay money to have it picked up. So they dump it in places like this."

"That's not fair!" shouted Wendy. "That means that no matter how many times we do this, the creek will never get clean! We might as well give up now."

"You'll never save this stream by giving up," Mrs. Asato pointed out. She began handing out garbage bags and rubber gloves. "Let's go, trash busters!" she said.

In spite of everything, everyone had a good time. As bag after bag of trash was filled, including two bags for the new paint cans, they really did feel as if they were making progress.

Steve was tired when he got home, but he couldn't rest. He had decided to write a letter to the *River City News* to tell the whole town about the illegal dumping.

Dear Editor:

My friends and I are in Mrs. Delgado's class at River City Elementary School. We have started a group called Save Our Stream to try to clean up Silver Creek.

Silver Creek was once a beautiful stream full of silver trout. Today it is full of garbage, and people are dumping more garbage every day.

We want to make Silver Creek clean again so it is healthy for fish and wildlife. We want everyone to stop polluting the stream and stop dumping their trash there.

Every Saturday is clean-up day at Silver Creek. We meet from 9 A.M.–11 A.M. Everyone is invited to come and help out, and WE NEED YOUR HELP if we're ever going to get Silver Creek cleaned up again.

Sincerely yours,

## Steve Alvarez

S.O.S.—Save Our Stream!

Steve sent the letter to the newspaper on Monday. He also sent a copy of the letter to the mayor of River City, but he wasn't sure if anyone would read it.

Someone did read the letter, though. On Friday morning, Steve came to school with the morning newspaper clutched in his hand. He opened it to the "Letters to the Editor" page.

"They printed my letter!" he shouted. The other kids gathered around to see. They were amazed. Now all they had to do was wait to find out if anyone who read their letter would help them.

# Chapter 6

# **Spreading the News**

The next day was Saturday, another cleanup day. Wendy's mother picked up the kids early to take them to the creek. Before they got in the car, Mrs. Asato gave them a surprise. She had made each of them a T-shirt with *S.O.S. Save Our Stream* written on the front. On the back was a picture of a fish splashing in water.

"These are great!" Steve said. "Thanks, Mrs. Asato!" He put on his shirt right away.

"A little publicity can't hurt," Mrs. Asato said, smiling at the kids in their new shirts.

What the kids didn't know was that they were about to get a lot more publicity. When they got to the creek, they were surprised. There were a lot of people there!

A woman with a microphone jumped out of a television news van when she saw the kids walking toward the trail that went down to the creek. Karen recognized her at once. "It's Tanya Lopez from TV news!" she yelled.

Tanya came up to Steve and the rest of the group. "You must be the kids from Save Our Stream," she said, nodding at their T-shirts.

"Are we going to be on TV?" asked Steve.

"Yes," said Tanya. "This clean-up idea of yours is a big story for River City. We're waiting for just one more person. There he is now."

It was the mayor of River City, Mayor Davis. He got out of a dark blue car and walked toward where Tanya and the kids were standing. The crowd gathered around.

"Where are the kids from Save Our Stream?" the mayor asked, looking around.

Steve and his friends stepped forward. Mayor Davis shook hands with all of them. The camera operator was taping the whole thing. There was a reporter and a photographer from the *River City News*, too.

"I read your letter," said Mayor Davis, "and I was very impressed. When I was a little boy, I caught my first fish in Silver Creek. My dad fished in the creek, too." Many people in the crowd nodded their heads. They remembered Silver Creek from when they were kids, too.

The mayor went on, "I think what you kids are doing is wonderful. Silver Creek is worth saving, and to show my support, River City is going to help. First of all, the City Parks Department will patrol the creek to stop people from dumping their trash here. Second, the City Sanitation Department will haul away the trash collected each Saturday. Finally, the City Police Department will enforce our laws against dumping. Anyone caught littering or dumping trash here will be fined $100.00."

The crowd cheered. Steve, Karen, Luke, and Wendy laughed. The photographer took a picture of the S.O.S. kids with the mayor.

Then the mayor rolled up his sleeves, put on a pair of rubber gloves, and headed down to the creek with everyone else. It was time to start the day's cleanup.

Tanya Lopez talked to the kids for a few more minutes. They introduced Mrs. Delgado and told the reporter all about how their teacher had taken them to the stream.

"Thanks for your time," Tanya told them as she and her crew packed up to leave. "Be sure to watch the six o'clock news tonight."

Sure enough, that night the story was on the six o'clock news. The news film showed the interview with the Save Our Stream group, then a shot of the mayor helping people pick up trash on the side of the creek. The next morning the kids were on the front page of the *River City News*. The headline read, *Mayor Helps Kids Clean Up Creek*, and under the story was their picture! It was probably the most exciting thing that had ever happened to them.

# Chapter 7

# More Good News

In the weeks that followed, Steve and his friends continued the Save Our Stream campaign and cleanup every Saturday. More and more people came to pick up trash and keep the creek clean.

The City Parks Department patrolled the creek, just as the mayor had promised they would. A few people were caught dumping trash late at night. Wendy, Steve, Karen, and Luke hoped the television news and front-page news story about the big fines the dumpers paid would be enough to stop anyone from ever dumping garbage in the creek again. Then the Parks Department placed DUMP NO CHEMICALS signs over the town's storm drains.

58

One Friday, Mrs. Delgado took her students to Silver Creek again. Everyone was excited to see the creek looking so clean as it flowed swiftly downstream.

"You've done a fantastic job cleaning up the creek," said Mrs. Delgado. "Unfortunately, it's still not clean enough for fish."

Mrs. Delgado leaned down and reached her hand into the water. She came up with a handful of gooey mud. "This dirt is called silt. It doesn't look harmful, but it is. When there's too much dirt in the water, the fish can't breathe. Dirt that settles on the bottom also buries fish eggs so they can't hatch. It can even bury the insects that fish eat."

"So what can we do?" Steve asked. "Can we take all the mud out of the creek?"

"Well, that wouldn't be practical," Mrs. Delgado answered. "There is a way to fix the problem, though. The stream needs more plants along its banks. Bushes and trees will prevent more dirt from sliding down into the stream when it rains. If we can keep new dirt from washing into the stream, the dirt that's already there will eventually settle down and become part of the normal riverbed."

"So let's get some plants," Karen said.

"Plants are expensive," Mrs. Delgado said. "I don't know where we could get enough money."

"I'll write the mayor another letter," Steve said, and that night he did.

Within a few days, the mayor called the school and talked to Mrs. Delgado. "Good news," she reported to the class. "The fine for dumping trash has been increased. The mayor says the money can be used for Silver Creek."

The following Saturday, instead of cleaning the creek, the S.O.S. kids and the other volunteers spent the day putting in new plants under the direction of the Parks Department.

It wasn't long before the creek was looking even better. Mrs. Delgado said it was time for the kids to collect water samples to test if fish could live in it. They sent a small sample of creek water to the Fish and Wildlife Division of the state Department of Environmental Protection.

On a warm Friday in June, Mrs. Delgado announced another field trip. When they got to the creek, they were surprised to see some people dressed in what looked like park ranger uniforms. There was also a tall woman in a bright blue suit.

Then Tanya Lopez arrived with a camera crew. "We're here today with Governor Parker as she makes a major environmental announcement for our state," Tanya said into her microphone.

One of the people whispered something to the governor, and she turned around. When she saw Mrs. Delgado's class, she came over.

"I can't thank you enough," she said, "for helping to save this precious natural resource, Silver Creek. Our fish and wildlife experts here tell me that fish can be reintroduced into the stream as early as this summer."

As Steve waited for his turn to shake the governor's hand, he thought back on the weeks of hard work. It had all started with one idea that seemed impossible. Wendy was right. Kids *can* do a lot!

# Glossary

**enforce**    [en FORS] to make people obey a rule or a law

**fertilizer**    [fur tul EYZ ur] chemicals or substances put in dirt as food for plants

**illegal**    [ihl LEE gul] not allowed by law; against the law

**litter**    [LIH tur] scraps of paper, cups, wrappers, and other garbage that is thrown on the ground

**motto**    [MAH toh] a brief saying used as a rule to live by

**pesticides**    [pes tuh SYDZ] any poisons used to kill insects and other pests

**polluted**    [puh LOO tud] made dirty or not pure; contaminated

**recyclable**    [ree SYK luh bul] can be used again

**resource**    [REE sors] a supply of something that can be used to meet a need

**toxins**    [TAHKS ihnz] poisons; harmful substances